H.o.r.s.e.

a game of basketball and imagination

CHRISTOPHER MYERS

EGMONT USA
NEW YORK

HEy, want to play a **game** of horse?

Yeah,

the game where one person
shoots any kind of shot —
layup, jumper from half-court,
bounce shot, whatever.

The other player has to
shoot the same shot, or else
that player gets a letter.

Spell "horse" and it's,
"Giddy-up, you're out."

Right, we call it "ghost"
where I come from. But the
game's the same.

You start.

Okay,
layup with
my eyes
closed.

waiT,
wait,
that's how you play?

That's just too easy;
we'll be here all day.

Oh, I was just starting easy.
I figured I'd give you a chance,
before you got horsed or ghosted
or whatever.

Don't be easy on me now.
Be easy on yourself.
Maybe you want to
practice a little
first.

I do not need practice to
beat some old "ghost" chump.

Why don't YOU start?

Okay, I'm going to stand here, at half-court, with my back to the hoop

and I'm going to skyhook this ball clear across the court into that basket,

with my eyes closed, standing on one foot, over my left shoulder.

Didn't know I could go left, did you?

You're probably a specialist in left ...
left back, left behind, left out.

Well, school is starting now.
Get a pencil, because I'm going first.

You see that building over there?

Waaaaay over there?

The white building?

No, the one next to it.

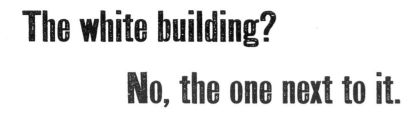

I can barely make out the windows.

Yep, that one.

I'm going to climb to
the roof of that building,

up 437

flights

of stairs.

$v_y = gt$

$y = \frac{1}{2}gt$

$a_x = 0$

v_{ox}

v_x

When I get there on the roof
of the building 437 stories high,
I will first calculate the wind speed
and direction, then, ever so carefully,

I will stand on one tiny tiptoe,
balance myself on the topmost corner
of the 437-story building,
and shoot a perfect layup,

with my left ...

foot.

That we could **leave** the court.

I didn't know that. If I'd known that,
I would've volunteered to go first ages ago.

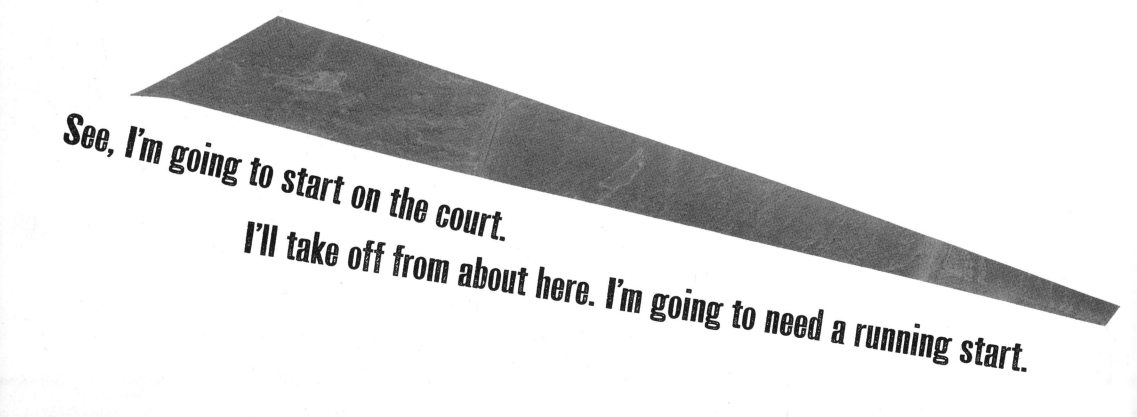

See, I'm going to start on the court.
I'll take off from about here. I'm going to need a running start.

I'm going to take off like a jet, leave the city, fly over buildings,

over the ocean, past Europe, over Africa and Asia, back through North America, one jump, clear around the world. I call this my Magellan shot. One jump (that is unless I get sidetracked by strong winds over the Pacific or something, then it'll be two jumps).

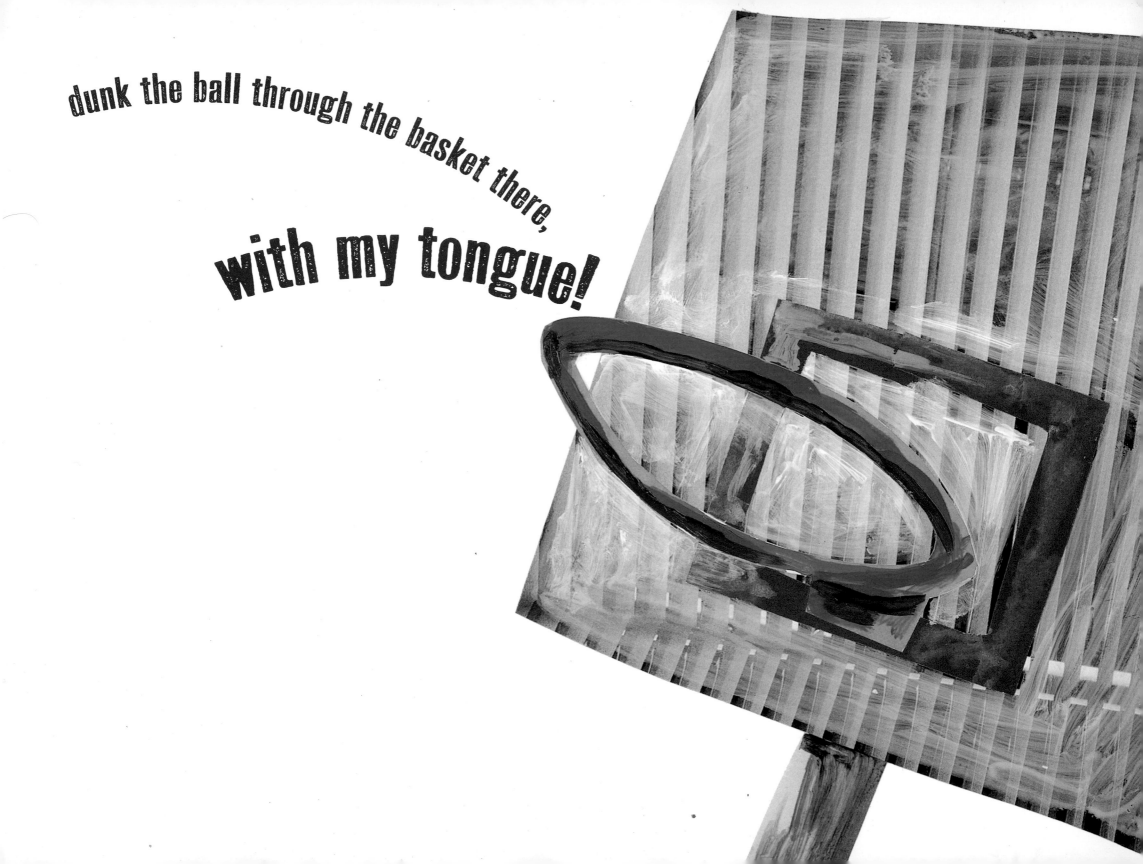

That's **not bad** for an amateur.

If you're as bad as you say you are, we can start where I usually start.

I'm glad you're thinking globally, because you're going to have to be in a planetary frame of mind to even understand what I'm going to do to start us off.

I'm going to need a special ball for this one.

It has to be
heat resistant,
cold resistant, and
space resistant.

That's right, I said it,
outer-space resistant!

It's kind of a bounce shot.

off the Moon, from there, the ball will ricochet through the vacuum of space,

astronomers will write articles asking,

"What is this new basketball-shaped comet?"

and come flying back to Earth, past the Moon, through the clouds,

That's not bad...
not bad at all.

EGMONT

We bring stories to life

First published by Egmont USA, 2012
443 Park Avenue South, Suite 806
New York, NY 10016

Copyright © Christopher Myers, 2012

All rights reserved

1 3 5 7 9 8 6 4 2

www.egmontusa.com

Library of Congress Cataloging-in-Publication Data

Myers, Christopher.

H.O.R.S.E. / Christopher Myers.

p. cm.

Summary: Two friends try to outdo each other on the basketball
court in an out-of-this-world game of H.O.R.S.E.

ISBN 978-1-60684-218-8 (hardback)

[1. Basketball–Fiction.] I. Title.

PZ7.M9825Hor 2012

[Fic]–dc23

2012003793

Designed by Yvette Lenhart

Printed in Shenzhen, China, by RR Donnelley

Author's Note

Kambui is my best friend. He's maybe one inch shorter than me, which still makes him pretty much taller than anyone you know. There're lots of wonderful things about him. When we first met, we talked about growing up in New York City and our favorite poets; we went to parties and danced like we had invented feet; we traded music and advice; we talked about how to make things. Kambui is a much better photographer than me, and I draw and paint better than he does. We teach each other and we learn from each other, like friends do.

And it's important to note he'll back me up on anything I say.

One day at a party in Brooklyn, there was a basketball court and a game broke out. We were on opposite teams, because we were the two tallest guys, and everyone said it wouldn't be fair if we were on the same team. It was a great game. It felt good to play against someone my size who wouldn't complain if I blocked his shots or bumped him. But also it felt good to play against someone who was an artist, because like dancing, sports can be as much about imagination as they are about athleticism.

When Kambui and I play against each other in basketball or in our summer touch football league with Hank and the rest of our artist crew, or Ping-Pong, we're not only playing with our bodies but also with our heads and hearts.

H.O.R.S.E. is a game like that, a game of imagination and skill, an anything-you-can-do-I-can-do-better contest. It's a game Kambui and I played as kids with our moms, dads, brothers, and sisters, the kind of thing that people can't complain about the unfairness of your being too tall, because it's not just about jumping up to touch the rim but about what kind of shots you can imagine doing. I've even played with my other best friend, Chitra. She is a foot shorter than me but has an amazing imagination. (Chitra is also a great artist.)

So this book is about my friends, the things we do together, our imaginations, and our athleticism. If you're lucky you have friends like mine. I'm sure you think you could beat us, but you would be wrong. The two main characters are me and Kambui as kids, and we've pretty much done every shot mentioned in the book.

If you don't believe me, ask him.